The New Zealand Cartel

Leilani Graceffa

First paperback edition October 2020

Book cover design by Leilani Graceffa

ISBN 978-1-7350952-6-4 (Paperback)
ISBN 978-1-7350952-7-1 (Hardcover)
ISBN 978-0-578-76251-7 (Ebook)

For more information, visit www.leilanigraceffa.com.

Olivia and Elliot and Sue and Jack—hello!

Chapter 1

I rub my ankle before handing Matthew's phone back to him. "How are we supposed to catch someone we haven't seen before, Matt?" I ask uneasily, still struggling to adjust to the four-inch stilettos firmly hugging my feet. "These shoes are already killing my feet."

"Sorry, Blake," He frowns, "those were all I could find in your size."

"It's okay. I'll switch them when we get inside." We have a general physical description of the guy from what we've been told, but there's no pictures or online profiles we can track and look at.

"Caroline gave us a physical description. We just have to keep our eyes open and watch for drugs being passed around."

"Okay." We don't have a high chance of catching him, but we'll go with this. "Hope for the best..."

He smiles warmly, "Prepare for the worst."

We both get out of the car, into the night's warm, autumn air, then enter the lobby of an opulent hotel. In a place like this, now we know this isn't just any kind of party. We will be surrounded by wealthy people, passing all types of drugs around. Expensive lightings and furniture everywhere, I'm beginning to think this drug lord we are looking for funded this gathering. Matthew checks us in, and knowing that we're not staying the night here, we walk up the staircase and head straight to the ballroom.

"Text me if you find anything."

The New Zealand Cartel

We split up, and I immediately go into a restroom to switch out the stilettos for my heeled flats and stuff them into my purse. Even though we are in an enormous ballroom almost jam-packed with people, Matthew and I seem to continuously cross and run into each other as we're searching. To avoid running into each other for the 50th time, I go out onto the balcony, leaving Matthew to cover the ballroom.

This balcony is vast, big enough to fit a good portion of the crowd in the ballroom. But there are only a few groups of people hanging out on it. And one of these groups contains a bunch of college students in a particular sorority. I hope they are not fixing to haze someone.

We're looking for a tall man with eyes a light shade of green, and he may or may not have facial hair. It could be anybody here; we recognize that.

After I text Matthew that the balcony is serene, I turn around and bump into a man who seems to be standing close behind me, assuming by the small gap between us. He quickly clutches me by the shoulders to help me regain my balance. "I'm sorry, sweetie," He apologizes without looking at me. He's looking in the direction of the college students in a far corner. This guy is tall, with a stubbled face. But he has brown eyes and isn't dressed in expensive attire like a typical wealthy person. I watch as he passes me and quickly makes his way to the corner group. Not the guy we're looking for.

I sit down onto a couch part of a dining set near the glass railing. Still texting Matthew back, and barely noticing the woman sitting across the table waiting for the guy to come back. When I eventually put my phone aside, she sees me appearing a bit bummed about this, so she decides to strike up a gentle conversation with me. Then the guy finally comes back and moves his canvas bag from beside me before sitting down and introducing himself to me as Brendan. She, Leslie. The three of us proceed to talk to each other for a while, almost making me forget that I am still on a mission.

Before I could ask them if they've seen the guy we're looking for, Matthew shows up from inside the ballroom to let me know that it's time to leave. We say our goodbyes, then Matthew and I leave the balcony.

"You get distracted too easily, Blake," Matthew affirms.

"I couldn't help it." I chuckle. "There wasn't much to pay attention to. Nothing was really happening. A group of college students were there though, I found that kind of weird."

"College students?"

"That's what I thought, at first." We didn't get to find the guy we're looking for, but at least we can say we tried. "And now I have to pee."

"Then go pee. I'll wait for you outside."

Once we get down the staircase, I leave Matthew's side and quickly go through a dimly lit hallway to eventually find a restroom. While I'm doing my business, I find my phone is not in my purse, and neither am I holding it in either of my hands. "My phone. My fucking..." I left it on the balcony. I hope Leslie and Brendan are still there.

After I wash my hands, I rush back up the staircase. As soon as I grab onto one of the doors handles to enter the ballroom, a pair of strong arms snatch me from behind. "HEY!" I start shouting and kicking. "LET ME GO! MATT—MATTHEW!" Another man appears from behind, approaching me holding an already needled and filled syringe in one of his hands.

❀❀❀❀❀

"Good morning..." I hear a voice say as I awake, immediately discovering my arms bound by rope to the headboard of a bed. And by the way it feels and seems like the bed is moving from underneath, it's not. We're on a plane. I turn my head towards where I heard the voice, finding a man standing before a bureau with his head lowered, not looking into the mirror in front of him. When he finally lifts his head, and I'm able to see his reflection in the mirror, I discover that he's not a stranger. Brendan. I don't return the greeting.

He smirks before taking off his glasses. "No?"

He set me up.

"Were you looking for your phone?" He asks, trying to get me to talk. I keep my mouth shut. So, he had my phone. "Oh, playing the silent treatment now, Auley? I'll get you to talk, detective."

He removes a pair of contacts from his eyes, revealing that his eye colour is actually a light shade of green. Instead of brown, like I saw when I first looked at him. The description Caroline gave to Matthew and me. He fooled us good. But how does he know that I'm a detective? I made sure not to let off much during that conversation. "How do you know?"

"Ahh, there's your voice." He smiles slyly. "You and your colleague arrested many of my traffickers. I knew you were looking for me."

He's the drug lord. He pulled a very convincing disguise, blending like a regular person at a party. I'm not sure why or how I never caught on to him, sitting beside him all that time. "So, you let your goons drug and abduct me?"

"Yes, but not because of that. I've been watching you for the last two years."

"And your point is?"

"What are they going to do without their foremost detective? You've caught too many of my people. The point is, I'm not letting you go, Blake." He frowns, "You're with me now."

What the...? No! "No, I'm not! Untie me!"

"No," He asserts almost aggressively, "even if I were to untie you, where will you go, who are you going to call? I don't have your phone anymore. I threw it off the balcony. And your gun, you won't be needing it anytime soon."

If he found my gun, which was in a holster strapped firmly to my upper leg underneath my dress, he must've looked up my dress while I was unconscious. "Did you at least keep my purse with my makeup remover?"

"Oh, I still have your purse. You just won't know where it is."

Had I paid close attention while on that balcony and not got distracted, I wouldn't be here. Matthew was right. I do get distracted too easily. He leaves for about a minute, returning with my bottle of liquid makeup remover and a few cotton rounds. "I think I can do it myself, thank you."

"Do you want me to untie you, or do you want your makeup off of your face?" He asks rhetorically.

"Both."

"I'm not untying you, sweetheart."

While he's wiping the makeup off my face, I notice he's holding something else in his hand. I continue to pay attention to it until he finishes, throws away the rounds, then opens his hand. It's my red lipstick. "Really?" I glare.

"It matches your red hair." He remarks with a smirk before getting uncomfortably too close to me. Then, he clenches my lower jaw to hold my head in place while applying it to my lips. "It's pretty on you."

I'm starting to think he kidnapped me for more than just to prevent getting caught and losing his empire. He seems like a creep. Didn't he just say he's been watching me for a couple of years? "You're creepy." Likely realizing that I'm catching on to his other possible plans for me, he keeps his mouth shut but lets a gentle but mischievous smile form on his face. I don't know, or even want to know, what kind of sick shit he has in mind, but it better not be what just crossed mine. "You better not be trying to rape me."

"I don't rape." The tone of his voice suddenly goes cold, "I don't hurt women."

"Then what the fuck was that smile for?"

"Don't worry about it. Thinking out loud." He turns around and walks back towards the bureau, grabbing something off of it. An already filled syringe. "That's enough questions."

Chapter 2

"Ow…" I wake up with a splitting headache, my arms now bound behind my back with something cold and metal. Probably handcuffs. I try to take a good look at the room in front of me. Besides the large desk a few feet away, I notice shelves on shelves full of books surrounding me, built into the walls, like a recently constructed library. But I know I'm far from being in a random library—rays of sunlight sprawl over me from a large, ceiling-height window behind this couch. Also, my clothes are missing.

So at this desk, appearing to be made from dark mahogany wood, Brendan sits behind an Apple laptop. "Good morning." He greets.

Again, I keep my mouth shut and don't return the greeting.

"You never return my greetings."

"I don't have to."

"You're going to have to start talking if you need me for anything."

"I don't need you for anything," I answer. "What I need you to do is to let me go."

"Geez, at least thank me for bathing you last night." He says, ignoring my plead.

What's this guy's problem and his motive for me? I roll my eyes, sighing, "Thank you."

"What I want you to do is be mine."

What the? What?! "I'm sorry,... excuse me?" He did all of this just to shoot his shot at me? "I have a man. No, thank you."

"But is he here?"

I turn my head to look at him, giving me a sly smirk from where he's sitting. "No, but y—"

"It's a rhetorical question, sweetheart." He interrupts.

"You're not going to make me cheat on him."

"I'm not planning on making you."

I'm going to be here for a while. I can tell. I might as well comply until I can contact Matthew or Interpol. "What are you planning on doing?"

"Don't worry about it." He answers before looking away. "Is he your partner?"

"Matthew? No, he's married. We're mutual."

I don't think I should've answered that. I still have that mischievous smile he gave me before in mind. "When are you going to untie me?"

"Don't be impatient. I'll do it on my own time."

He finishes whatever he's doing on his laptop. "Get up..." He almost commands, grabbing one of my arms and making me stand up from the couch. He holds onto my arm a bit firmly as he walks me into a different room, a bedroom. Its design is similar to his office, I'm guessing, the first room we were just in. The ceiling height windows and some but not as many built-in bookshelves, but the colour of the walls is... opaque. "This is where you'll be when I'm not here," He says, "and where you'll wait for me."

"Wait for you, for what?"

He withholds, not answering my question. With his grip still on my arm, he guides me towards the large, round bed, where he makes me kneel on my knees before the bed frame. Suddenly resting something lengthy on my right shoulder, he raises my head by my chin with it's soft, leathery tongue—a crop whip.

I know what this is.

"You will no longer be going by your name from here on..." He asserts.

I'm not sure if I can accept the name he wants me to go by in this particular situation because it's kind of inappropriate; it's a princess' name. Yes, my burgundy hair is his inspiration for it. I quickly decide to play along. I have no other choice. "Okay." I'm just going to say he wants to call me Ari. I wonder if he's making me use another name to keep me under his thumb, so CSIS and Interpol can't identify me. Or maybe I'm just thinking too deeply about this.

"I might just keep you." He says quietly but loud enough for me to hear.

What does he mean by that? I'm not going to bother asking him since he's most likely not going to tell me.

"I have a maid, her name is Giselle, and she will leave clothes for you every morning."

"Okay." As soon as I respond, I hear the sudden sound of his fly unzipping. I'm really regretting letting Matthew leave my side now.

I close my eyes. He makes me turn my head, and his "fun" with me begins.

At first, I resist opening my mouth to him. But upon realizing that he's likely not to let me go until I show him what I can do, I eventually let him in. He goes far into my throat, almost choking me. After a series of his moans and his session of face fucking me, he finally lets me breathe before releasing himself on my face.

Chapter 3

My body hurts. I need to find my purse. I'm not staying here; this guy is crazy.

All that choking and slapping and tying me up, he did. I'm pretty sure he choked me to sleep. I don't know what regular sex is anymore.

I sit up, finding the clothes Brendan promised his maid would bring me every morning, sitting folded at the end of the bed. A dress, but no bra and no panties... at least it's a pretty dress. "Nice." I crawl out of bed and find the bathroom. Yes, it's an oversized bathroom, to be exact.

It seems like his plan to kidnap me was premeditated for longer than two years, just by the way he has everything already set up for me. This dress is in my correct size, for God's sake. He did mention watching me, but I didn't think he meant this closely.

After I get done cleaning myself up and putting the dress on, I leave the bathroom and then begin to search around the bedroom for my purse. Eventually getting to the conclusion that it is not in this room. "Damn it." I sigh. He also said this is where I have to stay when he's not here.

He might not be here...

I rush towards the bedroom door, leaning in, trying to hear if Brendan or anybody is outside talking or something. I don't hear anything until I open the door, finding Brendan sitting at his desk writing something and a woman sitting in one of the chairs in front of the desk. The woman notices me first when she turns her head in my direction, and I immediately recognize her. I shut the door before Brendan can see me; if he hasn't already. "Jesus..."

I thought that woman was in jail? The last time I heard from my brother Issac, she got arrested for drug possession. How—What is she doing here? She's my niece's aunt, Joselyn. She is one evil bitch, hated even by her sisters, Laurie and Theodora.

Issac always had to fight her to keep her away from his daughter, Raelynn, because she is reportedly tied to a human trafficking ring as well.

I don't think he'll let me leave this room, especially not with her out there. And are these soundproof walls? I couldn't hear even a damn peep from outside until I opened the door.

"Come with me." I hear Brendan say as he gestures for me to come out and follow him. I do as he pleases. He makes me put on a pair of black ankle tied stilettos (also surprisingly in the correct size) with two-inch heels, what I can walk in comfortably. Compared to the four-inch pair I wore the other night. At this point, should I even be surprised if he knows my favourite food and brand of makeup?

After I finish tying the lace around my ankle, he pulls something black over my eyes, then ties it at the back of my head, blindfolding me. But why? He slips my arm between his, and we walk arm in arm to...somewhere. Somewhere where my nose quickly picks up the strong smell of gasoline. A garage?

He makes me lower my head to get into the passenger's seat of a car, and by the time I get my seatbelt to click, the engine of the car roars to life. "Mustang?" I don't know any other loud car engine better than a Mustang's. Matthew has one.

"Yes."

He eventually removes the blindfold from my eyes. I turn my head, taking in how island-like this place is; it's a gorgeous landscape with a fantastic view. But then I find out why it's island-like and where I am by looking up at one of the overhead highway signages: Greenhithe, Hauraki, Northcote Point... Auckland.

Leilani Graceffa

I'm in New Zealand.

We enter what I'm guessing is Auckland, with skyscrapers and expensive appearing boats and yachts in and surrounding the harbours. My sightseeing adventure ends when he drives into a parking garage; I'll see more when we leave. I wish I had my phone to take pictures.

This is another luxury hotel with a ballroom packed with people dressed opulently, compared to Brendan and me. But I guess dressing casually is the style he personally prefers and his way of hiding his wealth. I kind of like the way he outwardly portrays himself, even though he even had me fooled.

"Stay here." He says as he makes me sit down at a table away from the crowd.

He must know that I have a burner phone in my purse since he refuses to tell me where it is and likely won't let me take it anywhere if he were to.

So, as I'm sitting at this lonely table waiting for Brendan to come back, someone else—a man wearing a grey blazer, comes to sit down in the chair across the table. This man looks slightly similar to Matthew, but with more facial hair and his stoutly built figure, he appears scarier.

17

And yes, I'm implying that Matthew does look kind of scary because he rarely smiles and usually has a cold expression on his face.

But this man, when he raises his head to look at me, he actually gives me an earnest smile. "Hello."

"Hi," I smile back. Now I'm suspicious of him at first, as we begin to conversate—because this is almost exactly like how I got into this situation in the first place. But over time, I realize he seems generally interested in talking to me. I'm still keeping my guard up, though.

Brendan finally comes back while we're still talking. I immediately notice the sudden weird, dazed look in the man's eyes at him. "Oh..." He murmurs. "You're with Tristian."

Wait, his name is Tristian?

He looks at the man as if he recognizes him before quickly switching his gaze back to me. He extends his hand to me, helping me up from the chair.

So, I say goodbye, then Brendan (or Tristian, apparently) and I leave.

Leilani Graceffa

❀❀❀❀❀

He blindfolds me again before getting me out of the passenger seat and guiding me back inside and to his office. But he doesn't immediately remove the blindfold when we finally get there. He crosses my arms behind my back, then handcuffs my wrists together. "What are y—" I barely get my question out before getting muffled by something round with a silicone feeling, entering my mouth. A ball gag?

He pushes me down from behind, kind of forcing me to bend over onto a firm, smooth surface. His desk? Then he begins to slide my dress up over my butt, gently.

I quiver a bit when he starts touching me in that area, caressing me for a short amount of time before inserting a finger into me. Making me yelp, barely audibly. And he fingers me until he makes sure that I let out a moan or two, feeling myself throb down there as I attain an orgasm.

Chapter 4

I listened to his phone conversation with his mom while pretending to be asleep last night, so I kind of know what to expect today. He might be going to see his mom.

I'm still not giving up trying to find my purse. I've thoroughly searched this room, but not his office, yet. And I'm about to start doing that now if he's not in there currently. I put on another pretty, floral-patterned dress before slowly opening the door, finding him nowhere in sight. "Finally." Discovering that the room is empty, I begin to search around the office, eventually coming out empty-handed. "Damn it," I quietly curse to myself.

The one thing I did find is his name on his user account, on his laptop. His real name is Tristian. Brendan is a pseudonym, which makes sense.

So, as I'm just about ready to give up, I hear the door open, seeing Giselle holding folded clothes in her hands as she walks in. Just in time. "Giselle," I call out to her. "Do you know where Tristian hid my purse?"

She stays quiet for a second. I guess deciding whether she should tell me or not. "It's in the black safe under his desk."

There's a safe under the desk? I immediately rush back over to the desk to look under it. Yes, there is a black safe under it. "Do you know the combination?"

"I don't, sweetie."

"Shit!" I curse under my breath when we both begin to hear Tristian approaching, also hearing him talking to someone. I quickly crawl away from the desk, and Giselle continues doing her job before Tristian enters the room with a tall, older-looking woman with strawberry blonde hair.

"Here she is." He wraps his arms around me, hugging me, before kissing me on the forehead. I'm guessing this blonde woman is his mother. Is he pretending for her, or is he serious? "This is my girlfriend, Ariel."

I'm starting to hate this name solely because of this.

Am I supposed to pretend he didn't just kidnap me damn near a week ago? I force a smile, "Hello." I need to pretend anyway.

I'm now wondering if his mother secretly suspects or even knows Tristian is a drug lord and plays dumb when he says he's a doctor and works at a hospital. Yes, a doctor, since he allegedly has a doctorate. I don't know if doctors here in New Zealand get paid as much as he does trafficking drugs, but it's kind of unbelievable.

Just any old doctor probably wouldn't be able to afford a mansion like this.

"Thank you for keeping quiet." He says before kissing me on the cheek.

"You're a doctor?" I cross my arms, almost letting out a laugh. "Did you just lie to your mom?"

"Yes, I don't work at a hospital, but I do have a Doctorates degree. I am a doctor."

"And you're a drug lord, for what?"

"I used to be a prostitute and sold drugs to have a place to stay during my terms in University. My stepfather hated me, and he still does. He kicked me out of his house after I graduated secondary," He explains, "you can currently see where the rest of that lead to."

I see. I did not expect the first part. "You still love your mom after she let him kick you out?"

"It's not like she wanted him too. She secretly paid for my tuition with his money behind his back and sent me money when she could. I hate my stepfather, but why wouldn't I still love my mother?"

That's... sweet, but still kind of depressing. "Do you... not know your biological father or something?"

"I know him," He answers, "he died when I was a kid, and she eventually married my asshole stepfather."

"I know how that feels." Just his father dying part. But it wasn't our dad. It was our mom. "Can I ask one more question?"

"Sure."

"Your name is Tristian, not Brendan," I'm not going to mention seeing it as the name of his user account on his laptop, but... "That man I was talking to yesterday said it. You looked at him weirdly. Do you know him?"

He suddenly turns his head, staring at me with wide eyes, like he didn't expect me to ask that question. He purses his lips before slowly answering with, "That was my pimp."

Oh, my God. Oh, shit. I just went too deep. "Oh... I'm sorry for asking..."

"No, it's okay," He smiles gently, "it wasn't that bad."

23

I think I'm starting to get comfortable being here a little bit. Even without a phone to be able to contact anyone, I'm strangely finding this peaceful.

Instead of sitting and waiting around for what's to come next, I grab a pen and a sheet of printer paper before going outside onto the balcony to sit in one of the chairs, then start writing. Not writing random things, but a story, a story about what I've experienced so far. Not only to pass the time but for my brother, Issac. He's a writer and an author of many great romance novels. I'm sure my situation could probably spark an idea and inspire a future story for him. If I ever get to see him again.

"Hey," I hear Tristian from behind as I'm writing.

For the first time since I've been here, I return his greeting, "Hi."

"Are you writing?"

"Yeah..." I answer, "I can't write a story?"

"Is it for your brother?"

Damn it, he knows. "How much do you know about me, exactly?"

He doesn't answer my question, as always, when I ask something too revealing. "I know your older brother is a famous author."

I hope he didn't do all of this just for this. "That's nice. Go buy one of his books."

"I already have most of them."

Ah, he must be a reader and loves to read. Now all of the books and the bookshelves make sense. "Did you kidnap me just for this?"

"No," He replies. "I don't want to hurt you. I don't want anything from you."

Then why... never mind. I might as well not ask. "Okay."

"I love you, Blake."

I immediately drop my pen. He what...? How, why? We barely know each other. Well, I'm stuck here, and I know I will be for a while, so I guess I'll go with it. I damn so don't love him back, but I have to keep up the act. I stay quiet for at least a minute, thinking of how to answer him before responding with, "I don't love you, but I like you."

He takes my response well, unexpectedly. Letting a soft smile come across his face. "I appreciate your honesty."

Chapter 5

I'm pretty sure I've been here for almost a month, or maybe more than a month, now that I think about it. I haven't been counting the days. I should ask Tristian for today's date after I put my dress on.

Everything is still and quiet, as usual early in the morning here, until I come out of the bathroom after showering to put on my dress. I stop in my tracks before even approaching the bed, hearing the drowned out voice of someone yelling outside of the room. I turn towards the door, taking a few steps closer to it, noticing that the voice yelling is Tristian's. Most likely cursing someone out.

Before I can grab the handle of the door, it swings open, and Tristian rushes in towards me, clearly enraged. "Get in the bed!" He snarls before clutching me by my shoulders.

Startled, I anxiously ask, "For what?"

"GET IN THE BED!" He's holding something long and transparent in one of his hands... a syringe. He quickly uncaps it, piercing one of my arms with its needle.

The

New Zealand

Cartel (Part 2)

Leilani

Graceffa

Chapter 1

"You think you'll be able to do this one, Blake?" Caroline asks. "If you don't think so, just say no."

"Yeah, I can do it."

"Are you sure?"

"Yes." Caroline is asking now because this is my first mission back on the job since I've been out for seven months, pregnant and sick. Then I took two and a half months off after giving birth to take care of my baby. Yes, Tristian got me pregnant, though I don't believe it was intentional. I found out after being tested for STDs and STIs.

Matthew arrested one of his people. They ratted Tristian out but didn't reveal his real name and gave Matthew one of his pseudonyms instead. They raided his mansion, found me lying unconscious in Tristian's bed, but couldn't find him anywhere. Someone must've alerted him ahead of time. He vanished; they never found him.

"How's Andy, Blake?" Matthew asks.

"He's doing great," I answer, "he's with my brother." Andy is my baby boy, and Matthew insisted on naming him that. I broke my relationship with my ex-boyfriend off, so Matthew, even though he's married and has his own family, was there for me throughout my pregnancy. Holding Andy as if he was one of his own children was the first time I've ever seen him smile so big.

I thought of putting him up for adoption, at first. But I wouldn't let him leave my arms after they gave him to me.

This case involves someone we can actually track down by their appearance, and they're involved in a child sex trafficking ring. And Caroline advised me to stay by Matthew's side this time, which I will definitely be doing. I won't be surprised if this has to do with the remainder of Joselyn's people. I heard Theodora, Laurie, and her son, Ian, threw a monkey wrench in her trafficking venture in Alberta, right after Tristian got raided. Apparently, they aired her dirty laundry out too. "Where are we going?"

"This guy works at an adult bookstore downtown Halifax. All we have to do is find and arrest him." Matthew explains. "If there's not more of them. We already arrested most of them while you were out."

"An adult bookstore? Isn't that..."

"Obvious? Very."

Having this case, ironically, after becoming a mother. Child molesters have always nauseated me, but now I hope they all endure slow and painful deaths when it's time for them to burn in hell, along with the rest of the scum that was once alive.

The New Zealand Cartel (Part 2)

"Seen him?" Matthew asks the woman behind the checkout counter, showing her a picture on his phone.

"Andrew? He's the manager. He's in the back."

We enter the stockroom, quickly scanning through the many aisles for this guy, but finding nobody. "That door," I point at a door near us, held cracked open by something set between it and the door frame. I open it, finding an empty parking lot with two men standing in the middle of it, talking. The two men notice, turning their heads to look at us, before booking it.

We run after them. Matthew, who's the fastest out of both of us, catches up to one of them, snatches the back of his shirt, then pins him against a wall. I continue to chase the guy we were looking for in the first place down a couple more blocks, until he suddenly stops, then turns around with a pistol in one of his hands.

Bad timing. He grabs ahold of me before I can turn around to run away, aiming the barrel of the gun at my temple as Matthew hastily approaches.

"Put the gun down, man."

Matthew's eyes shift away from us, looking at something, or someone, behind the man. He nods his head slowly.

POP His hold on me looses, then both of his arms fall. I rush over into Matthew's arms before the man's body collapses onto the pavement.

"Who are you?" Matthew asks.

I turn my head to look at the person. "Tristian..."

"Tristian Taylor," He answers. "You must be Mateo Torres."

Chapter 2

"He's beautiful." Tristian smiles at the cooing infant in his arms.

He tracked me down using my old driver's license that was in my purse after figuring out he got me pregnant when he saw Issac's social media post about me.

He doesn't want to leave me alone to raise Andy by myself... and wanted to return my purse.

I never told anybody his real name when they asked. Hopefully, nobody will figure out he was the drug lord that kidnapped me.

www.ingramcontent.com/pod-product-compliance
Lightning Source LLC
Chambersburg PA
CBHW020144150626
46552CB00021B/1644